The Big Game

by Michèle Dufresne
Illustrated by Sterling Lamet

Contents

Literacy Footprints, Inc.

Chapter 1
The Players

Little Dinosaur was excited.

Today was the big game between

his baseball team, the Jungle Warriors,

and Bully Dinosaur's team,

the Thunder Bangers.

When Little Dinosaur got to the dugout,

he looked around and saw a lot of

sad and worried faces.

"What's wrong?" he asked Monkey.

"Why is everyone looking so worried?"

2

"Betty Badger and her brother Billy Badger are sick," said Monkey. "And Walter Walrus is on vacation with his family. We don't have enough of a team to play. We are going to have to forfeit the game!"

"This is a bummer," said Harry the Hippo. "We worked so hard to get to the playoffs!"

Just then Baby Stegosaurus
and Baby Tiger walked into
the dugout. "Hi," said Baby Tiger.
"We just came by to wish you good luck.
We know you are going to be great."

"Well, thanks, but it looks like there
isn't going to be a game,"
said Little Dinosaur.

"Why not?" asked Baby Stegosaurus.
"What's happened?"

"We don't have enough players,"
said Little Dinosaur.

Baby Stegosaurus and Baby Tiger
looked at each other.
"*We* could play," they said.

"What?" cried Monkey. "You're too little!
You can't play!"

Little Dinosaur said, "Monkey,
if Baby Tiger and Baby Stegosaurus
don't play, then we can't
have the game!"

"Yeah," said Harry the Hippo.
"I say let them play."

Chapter 2
New Team Members

Monkey took off his baseball hat and scratched his head.
"All right, but I'm sure we'll lose," he said.

"Well, I'm not sure we want to play then," said Baby Tiger.

"Please play," said Harry the Hippo. "We really need you."

"Well . . ." said Baby Stegosaurus.

He looked at Baby Tiger.

"If you help us out, we will do anything you ask in return," said Little Dinosaur.

"Monkey will do anything we want?" asked Baby Tiger.

Monkey sputtered,
"I don't think . . ."

"Yes," said Little Dinosaur.
"And Monkey, too! Right, Monkey?"

The whole team looked at Monkey.

Monkey said, "Okay. Me, too."

Soon it was time for the game
to begin. The Thunder Bangers were up
at bat first. Little Dinosaur was
the team pitcher.

The bases were loaded
when Bully Dinosaur came up to bat.

"I'm going to hit a home run.
The score will be four to zip,"
said Bully Dinosaur.

Little Dinosaur looked around.
Baby Tiger and Baby Stegosaurus
were in the outfield. Little Dinosaur knew
Bully could hit a home run. Bully was
a great hitter.

"We can get the ball!"
said Baby Tiger.
"Go ahead and pitch," she called
to Little Dinosaur.

Little Dinosaur threw the ball.
It went whizzing to the left
of the plate.

"Ball one!" called the umpire.

Little Dinosaur threw another ball.

"Ball two!" called the umpire.

"Hey, you little chicken," said Bully.
"Are you trying to walk me
so I don't hit a home run?"

"Chicken, chicken!" called Bully's team.
"Little Dinosaur is a chicken!"

Chapter 3
The Big Hit

Monkey ran up to Little Dinosaur.
"Don't listen to them," he whispered.
"Walk him. We don't want him to get
a hit out to the outfield.
Baby Tiger and Baby Stegosaurus
will never be able to catch the ball."

Baby Tiger seemed to know
what Monkey was telling Little Dinosaur.
"Come on, Little Dinosaur.
Let him hit the ball.
We'll catch it!" she called to him.

Little Dinosaur wasn't sure what to do.

Should he let Bully walk?

Should he try to get him to strike out?

He wasn't sure what to do!

What would be best?

"Throw the ball!" shouted Bully Dinosaur.

Little Dinosaur threw the ball. Slam!
Bully whacked the ball and it flew
to the outfield. Little Dinosaur watched
Baby Tiger jump up with her glove
and catch the ball.

She threw it to Baby Stegosaurus.
Baby Stegosaurus tagged the
Thunder player running to third base.
Then he threw the ball to second base.
Monkey caught the ball and tagged
a Thunder player running
from first to second base.

"Three outs!" called the umpire.

"A triple play! Hooray!"
cried all the Jungle Warriors.

At the end of the game, the score was five to two. The Warriors won the game! The team jumped up and down.

"Great game, thanks to Baby Stegosaurus and Baby Tiger!" said Little Dinosaur. "Now we need to do something for them, just like we promised."

Baby Tiger looked at Baby Stegosaurus.

They both had big smiles.

"We want to do stuff with you," she said.

"Yeah," said Baby Stegosaurus.

"Like, when you go fishing.

We want to go!"

"Oh, boy," groaned Monkey.

"We should have forfeited the game!"